Short-Short Stories

Compiled by
Jean Warren

Illustrated by Marion Hopping Ekberg
Activity Illustrations by Paula Inmon

Warren Publishing House, Inc.
Everett, Washington

Thanks to all the TOTLINE subscribers who submitted stories to our short story contest, and special thanks to those whose stories appear in this book.

Editor: Elizabeth S. McKinnon
Production Editors: Brenda Mann Harrison
                     Gayle Bittinger
Cover Design: Larry Countryman

ISBN 0-911019-13-8

Library of Congress Catalog Card Number 86-051509
Printed in the United States of America

Contents

Introduction

"Stories are the sunshine that turn a child's imagination into rainbows." — *Sharon Creeden*

Stories provide delightful ways for children to learn. While coloring their imaginations, stories teach children new ideas, expand their language skills and stimulate their creativity. This is particularly true for young children, who need a variety of stories that are appropriate for their age level and that help them learn about themselves and about the world around them.

The 18 stories in this book have been written or adapted especially for preschool-aged listeners. The stories are short and easy to understand, thus promoting successful learning experiences. With their seasonal themes, the stories combine appropriateness with enjoyment to make them favorites that can be read over and over again throughout the year.

To aid in developing listening skills, each story is accompanied by just one illustration. Because the illustrations show only the story characters, the children are left free to use their imaginations to supply the story actions. Later, when the children have become familiar with the storylines, they can use the illustrations as reminders when recreating the stories in their own words.

Following each story are two pages of extended activities, which include a song, an art activity, a snack recipe and a game or other learning activity. These activities, many of which have been selected and adapted from other Totline sources, are designed to help you integrate the stories into a number of different learning areas.

We have truly enjoyed putting the stories together for this book. It is our hope that you will find them to be useful teaching tools and that they prove to be sunshine that turns your children's imaginations into rainbows.

Jean Warren

Apple Man's Secret

By Jean Warren

Sarah loved having Grandma come to visit. They always had fun making things together.

Today Sarah helped Grandma pick apples from the old apple tree. Then together they made two large apple pies and ten small jars of applesauce. When they were done, they had one large apple left.

"I know," said Grandma. "Let's make an Apple Man."

Grandma took out some whole cloves and some toothpicks from her cupboard. She showed Sarah how to stick the cloves into the apple to make two eyes, a nose and a mouth. Then she showed Sarah how to stick toothpicks into the apple to make arms for the Apple Man.

Sarah was delighted with her new apple friend. They played together for the rest of the day. Sarah even took Apple Man upstairs when she went to bed. And before she fell asleep, she shared a secret with her apple friend.

"I have a new baby brother," Sarah whispered to Apple Man. "His name is Andrew, and my parents are bringing him home from the hospital tomorrow."

In the morning Sarah told Grandma about sharing her secret with Apple Man.

"You know what?" said Grandma. "Apple Man has a secret, too. He has a secret inside of him that he would like to share with you."

Sarah loved secrets. What could it be, she wondered.

Grandma cut Apple Man in half, right across the middle. And there inside was Apple Man's secret — a beautiful little star!

"Oh," cried Sarah, "what a wonderful surprise! Thank you, Apple Man, for sharing your secret with me. I wish I could share it with Baby Andrew."

"I know," said Grandma. "Let's make a star picture for Andrew's room."

Grandma found a large sheet of paper and some paints. Next, she put a sponge on a small plate and poured some paint on the sponge. Then she showed Sarah how to dip half of the apple into the paint and then press the apple on the paper to create a beautiful star print.

Sarah printed stars all over the paper. Her picture was finished by the time her parents arrived home with Baby Andrew.

Sarah loved her new brother. "Someday," she thought, "I'm going to make an Apple Man for Andrew. And someday, just like Grandma told me, I'm going to tell him about Apple Man's secret."

Extended Activities
Apple Man's Secret

DO YOU KNOW THE APPLE MAN?
Sung to: "The Muffin Man"

Do you know the Apple Man,
The Apple Man, the Apple Man?
Do you know the Apple Man
Who likes to play with me?

Oh, he has a great big smile,
A great big smile, a great big smile.
Oh, he has a great big smile
And likes to play with me.

Oh, he has a bright red face,
A bright red face, a bright red face.
Oh, he has a bright red face
And likes to play with me.

Oh, he has a star inside,
A star inside, a star inside.
Oh, he has a star inside
And likes to play with me.

Let the children make up other verses.

Jean Warren

APPLE STAR PRINTS

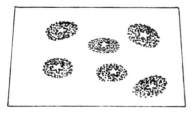

MATERIALS: Construction paper; apples; red, yellow and green tempera paint; shallow containers; sponges; paper towels; knife.

PREPARATION: Cut apples in half crosswise. Blot the cut surfaces with paper towels and let the apples dry for about an hour. Place sponges (or folded paper towels) in shallow containers and pour on tempera paints.

ACTIVITY: Have the children dip the cut surfaces of the apples into paint and then press them on their papers to make star prints.

APPLESAUCE

3-4 sweet apples
1/2 cup water

1/2 teaspoon cinnamon

Quarter, core and peel the apples. Cut each quarter section in half and put all the apple pieces into a saucepan. Add water and sprinkle on cinnamon. Simmer, covered, until tender (about 20 minutes). Let the children mash the cooked apples with a potato masher or whirl the apples in a blender. Let cool before serving.

Makes 6 small servings

APPLE MAN PUPPET FUN

MATERIALS: A large apple; whole cloves; toothpicks; carrot curls (optional); tape recorder or large sheets of paper and crayons; stapler (optional).

PREPARATION: Use the apple to make an Apple Man puppet. Stick whole cloves into one side of the apple to make two eyes, a nose and a mouth. Stick toothpicks into the apple on either side of the face to make arms. Use toothpicks to attach carrot curls for hair, if desired.

ACTIVITY: Let the children take turns holding the Apple Man puppet and making up stories about his adventures. Record the stories on tape for later listening. Or write down each child's story on a large sheet of paper for him or her to illustrate. If desired, staple the illustrated stories together with a cover to make an Apple Man book.

The Giant Pumpkin

By Jean Warren

Early one morning when the sun burst out,
A little white seed began to sprout.

She pushed her head up through the ground,
Waved her arms and looked around.

At first she grew low, but she was vine,
So soon she began to climb and climb.

She climbed up a hill, to the very top,
And there at last she decided to stop.

From the vine popped a flower, a great
  big one,
As gold as the color of the setting sun.

The vine was happy, but then one day,
The beautiful flower fell away.

Then the vine grew sad, she felt real low,
Until a green ball began to grow.

It grew and it grew to a great big size,
Then it turned all orange — a big surprise!

Way up high at the top of the hill,
The giant pumpkin sat very still.

He saw some children playing below
And wished that down the hill he could go.

He leaned to the left, and he leaned to
  the right.
He pushed and pushed with all his might.

He kept on leaning and pushing until
He started to roll right down the hill.

He rolled and rolled, first slow, then fast,
Until the children he reached at last.

The children took the pumpkin to the
  county fair
Where he won a blue ribbon that he
  could wear.

They said he was bigger than all the rest,
That of all of the pumpkins, he was the best.

The pumpkin felt proud, and he wanted
  to grin.
(It's not every day that a ribbon you win!)

So the children carved him a smile big
  and wide
And gave him a candle to glow inside.

Now that pumpkin's as happy as can be,
For he's a jack-o'-lantern for all to see!

Extended Activities
The Giant Pumpkin

I'M A GIANT PUMPKIN
Sung to: "I'm a Little Teapot"

I'm a giant pumpkin,
Orange and round.
   (Hold arms in circle above head.)
When I'm sad,
My face wears a frown.
   (Frown.)
But when I am happy, all aglow,
Watch my smile just grow and grow!
   (Smile.)

Repeat, substituting the words "little pumpkin" for "giant pumpkin."

Barbara Hasson
Portland, OR

PAPER BAG PUMPKINS

MATERIALS: Paper lunch bags; twist ties; newspaper; orange and green tempera paint; brushes; paint containers; green yarn.

PREPARATION: Pour paint into paint containers and set out all materials.

ACTIVITY: Have the children tear newspaper into scraps and use them to stuff their paper lunch bags. Secure each bag with a twist tie, leaving about 1 inch of the bag gathered at the top. Then have the children paint the bottom parts of their bags orange and the gathered parts green to create pumpkins with stems. When the pumpkins have dried, string them all together with a green yarn "vine" to make a "pumpkin patch."

SENT IN BY: Cathy Griffin, Princeton Junction, NJ

12

JACK-O'-LANTERN SANDWICHES

Whole-wheat bread slices   Mayonnaise
Cheese slices

For each sandwich, cut a smiling jack-o'-lantern face out of a slice of bread. Spread mayonnaise on another slice of bread, lay a cheese slice on top and cover with the slice of bread from which you have cut out the jack-o'-lantern face. (If desired, use egg salad instead of cheese slices.)

CREATIVE MOVEMENT FUN

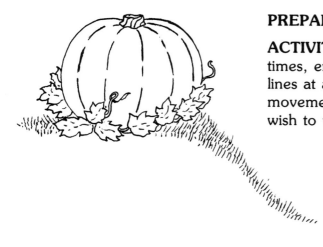

MATERIALS: None.

PREPARATION: None.

ACTIVITY: After reading *The Giant Pumpkin* aloud several times, encourage the children to act out the story. Read two lines at a time and let the children experiment with different movements. Since the story is divided into two parts, you may wish to use it for two separate movement activities.

Better Silly Than Sorry

By Ellen Javernick, Loveland, CO

Richard had on his clown suit. He had a white face and a big red nose. He even had orange hair! He and Mother were going to drive to Grandpa's house so Grandpa could see how Richard looked in his Halloween costume.

"May I take Jack to Grandpa's, too?" asked Richard.

"That's a good idea," said Mother.

Richard ran back into the house to get Jack. Jack was his jack-o'-lantern — a big orange pumpkin with a silly grin. Jack had only three teeth.

Richard and Mother climbed into the car. Mother buckled her seat belt. Richard slid over close to Mother and buckled his seat belt, too, all by himself.

Richard put Jack on his lap. Then he said, "Wait, Mom. I just remembered something. It's not safe to ride on someone's lap. It's not safe to ride in a car without a seat belt. Something might happen to Jack if I don't buckle him up."

Mother smiled. "You're right," she said. "Everyone should wear a seat belt when riding in a car. You can fasten the seat belt that's next to the door around Jack."

Richard put Jack beside him on the car seat. Then he slipped the seat belt around the big orange pumpkin and snapped the belt in place. Jack looked a little silly.

"Better silly than sorry," said Mother.

Soon Mother, Richard and Jack were driving to Grandpa's. Then just as they turned a corner, a black cat ran across the street.

Mother quickly put on the brakes. The car came to a screeching stop. Mother's seat belt pulled tight, and so did Richard's. Jack rolled a little, and his face bumped against the door handle. But his seat belt pulled tight, too, and he stayed in the car seat beside Richard.

"Whew!" said Mother. "That was lucky. We could have been badly hurt if we hadn't been wearing our seat belts. I'm glad that Jack had his seat belt on, too. Otherwise he might have been smashed and splashed all over everything."

Richard, Mother and Jack drove the rest of the way to Grandpa's house. Grandpa was glad to see them. He was happy that no one was hurt when the car stopped so suddenly.

"It looks like Jack's teeth got a little loose when he bumped against the door handle," said Grandpa. "I'll get some rubber bands and some wire, and we'll make Jack some braces. Then his loose teeth won't fall out while he's grinning the night away.

"I'm glad that Jack is here to celebrate Halloween with us," Grandpa added. "I'm glad he was wearing a seat belt!"

Extended Activities
Better Silly Than Sorry

BUCKLE UP
Sung to: "A-Hunting We Will Go"

The wheels go round and round.
   (Move arms in circles.)
We drive the car in town.
   (Pretend to steer car.)
We buckle up so if we stop,
   (Pretend to fasten seat belt.)
We'll all be safe and sound.
   (Cuddle self with arms.)

The wheels go round and round.
   (Move arms in circles.)
We drive Jack 'round the town.
   (Pretend to steer car.)
We buckle him up so if we stop,
   (Pretend to fasten Jack's seat belt.)
Jack will be safe and sound.
   (Pretend to cuddle Jack.)

Judy Hall
Wytheville, VA

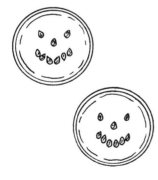

PLAYDOUGH JACK-O'-LANTERNS

MATERIALS: Plastic lids; orange playdough; sunflower seeds (unshelled).

PREPARATION: To a batch of playdough (made from your favorite recipe or from the recipe below), add drops of red and yellow food coloring to make orange.

ACTIVITY: Have the children press orange playdough into their plastic lids. Then let them press sunflower seeds into the playdough to create jack-o'-lantern faces. When the playdough has dried, remove the jack-o'-lanterns from the plastic lids, if desired.

PLAYDOUGH RECIPE: From Mrs. David Zucker, Reno, NV
Mix together 1 cup flour, 1/2 cup salt, 3 to 4 tablespoons water and 1 tablespoon vegetable oil. Add a few drops of food coloring as desired.

BANANA PUMPKIN FOAMIES

1 cup milk   1 banana, sliced
2 tablespoons canned pumpkin   Dash of cinnamon

Put all ingredients into a blender container and blend until thick and foamy. Pour into paper cups.

Makes 2 4-ounce servings

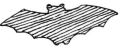

HALLOWEEN SHAPES GAME

MATERIALS: Colored construction paper; pair of scissors.

PREPARATION: Cut a set of different Halloween shapes out of colored construction paper (a white ghost, an orange pumpkin, a black witch's hat, a brown owl, etc.). If you have a large group of children, make several sets of shapes.

GAME: Have the children sit in a circle and give a Halloween shape to each child. Then sing the song below and have the children holding the appropriate shapes respond to the directions.

Sung to: "The Muffin Man"

Oh, do you have the (spooky ghost/orange pumpkin/etc.),
The (spooky ghost/orange pumpkin/etc.),
The (spooky ghost/orange pumpkin/etc.)?
If you have the (spooky ghost/orange pumpkin/etc.),
Please (hold it up high/stand up and bow/etc.).

Continue singing the song until you have mentioned all of the shapes. Then let the children exchange shapes and start the game again. Continue playing as long as interest lasts.

SENT IN BY: Barbara H. Jackson, Denton, TX

Running Bear's Thanksgiving

By Jean Warren

Running Bear was happy. Today was Thanksgiving, and he had been invited to a big celebration that was being given by his friends, the Pilgrims.

Everyone was going to take food to the celebration to share. Running Bear wished that he was old enough to go hunting. Then he could take a wild turkey or some venison to the celebration. But he was still a boy. Instead, he decided to take a basket of nuts that he had gathered and dried.

Running Bear dressed in his finest buckskin clothes. He put the basket of nuts in his canoe. Then he climbed into the canoe and began paddling down the river.

When Running Bear came close to the Pilgrims' settlement, he saw many of his friends standing on the riverbank, waving. He was so excited that he stood up to wave back. But as he stood, the canoe tipped down into the water, and out fell Running Bear and the basket of nuts with a big splash!

Running Bear was a good swimmer. He grabbed hold of the canoe, which had tipped back up again, and pulled it to shore.

Running Bear's friends were glad to see that he was all right. But Running Bear was sad. The basket of nuts he had brought with him was gone.

"I'm sorry, friends, but I have no food to share with you for our Thanksgiving celebration," he said.

"What do you mean?" his friends cried. "You have brought the best food of all. Just look in your canoe!"

Running Bear looked down into his canoe. And there, to his surprise, was a great big fish!

Running Bear was happy again. He had something to share with his friends at Thanksgiving after all.

Extended Activities
Running Bear's Thanksgiving

HURRAY, IT'S THANKSGIVING DAY!
Sung to: "When Johnny Comes Marching Home"

The Pilgrims are coming to celebrate,
Hurray! Hurray!
The Pilgrims are coming to celebrate
Thanksgiving Day.
The Pilgrims are coming, so don't be late,
We'll eat and dance to celebrate.
And we'll all be glad, so
Hurry and don't be late!

The Indians are coming to celebrate,
Hurray! Hurray!
The Indians are coming to celebrate
Thanksgiving Day.
The Indians are coming, so don't be late,
We'll eat and dance to celebrate.
And we'll all be glad, so
Hurry and don't be late!

Additional verses: "Running Bear's coming to celebrate;
(Child's name) is coming to celebrate."

Jean Warren

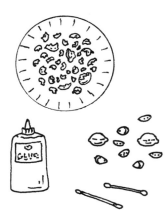

NUTSHELL COLLAGES

MATERIALS: Small paper plates or squares of lightweight cardboard; nutshells; Q-tips; glue; small containers.

PREPARATION: Save the shells from a variety of nuts you have cracked. Break the shells into different-sized pieces. Pour glue into small containers.

ACTIVITY: Have the children use Q-tips to dab generous amounts of glue on their paper plates or cardboard squares. (Older children can squeeze on drops of glue directly from the bottles.) Then let the children place broken nutshell pieces on top of the glue to make nutshell collages.

CORN BREAD

1 cup flour
1 cup yellow cornmeal
1/2 teaspoon salt
1 tablespoon baking powder
1/2 cup apple juice concentrate

1 egg
1/2 cup milk
1/4 cup vegetable oil
1 banana, sliced

Stir dry ingredients together in a bowl. Blend remaining ingredients in a blender and add this mixture to the dry ingredients. Pour into a greased 9-inch baking pan and bake at 400 degrees for 25 to 30 minutes.

Makes 16 small squares

THANKSGIVING FEATHER GAME

MATERIALS: A large paper sack; assorted colors of construction paper; pair of scissors.

PREPARATION: Cut feather shapes out of a variety of colored construction paper. Put feather shapes into the paper sack.

GAME: Have the children sit in a circle. Let one child at a time reach into the paper sack and take out a feather. Explain that in order to keep the feather, the child must name something he or she is thankful for that is the same color as the feather (blue sky, red apples, my brown dog, etc.). Continue the game as long as desired, making sure that everyone ends up with the same number of feathers.

The Bear and the Mountain

By Jean Warren

There once was a mountain,
So big and so tall,
Who lived all alone
With no friends at all.

He smiled at planes
High in the sky.
But none of them stopped
As they flew by.

All through the winter
He was covered with snow.
Then during the summer,
Wildflowers would grow.

He often saw people,
Who came just to play.
But none of them ever
Wanted to stay.

They all were too busy,
Too much on the go.
Up they would climb,
Then down they would flow.

Then one fine day
Something panted and sighed
As it huffed and it puffed
Up the mountain's side.

Slowly up the mountain
Came a little brown bear,
Wearing wildflowers
In her soft, fuzzy hair.

"Hello, Big Mountain!
How do you do?
Can I please spend
This summer with you?"

"Of course," said the mountain.
"It will be fun.
Run all you like
On my tummy-tum-tum."

Little Bear was happy.
The mountain was, too.
Having a friend
Was something quite new.

Little Bear would race
Up the mountain's side.
Then down she would tumble
And slip and slide.

All through the summer
Their friendship grew.
But then one day
The cold winds blew.

Now Little Bear knew
That she had to go
Before the mountain
Was covered with snow.

"Please don't go!"
The mountain cried.
"I'll make a safe place
Where you can hide."

He rumbled and rolled,
Then cupped his arm
To make a warm cave,
All safe from harm.

Now Little Bear
Had a cozy new home.
Now never again
Would she have to roam.

Let the snow come —
She didn't care.
She had a home
Just right for a bear.

The bear and the mountain
Were a sight to see,
Together as friends,
Living happily.

Extended Activities
The Bear and the Mountain

BEARS ARE SLEEPING
Sung to: "Frere Jacques"

Bears are sleeping, bears are sleeping
   (Pretend to sleep.)
In their lairs, in their lairs.
Soon it will be springtime,
Soon it will be springtime.
Wake up, bears! Wake up, bears!
   (Pretend to wake up.)

Joyce Marshall
Whitby, Ontario

FUZZY BROWN BEARS

MATERIALS: Brown paper grocery sacks; used tea bags (dried); pair of scissors; brushes; glue; small cups; large box lids; buttons or circle stickers.

PREPARATION: For each child, cut a bear shape out of a brown paper sack. Cut open the tea bags and put the tea leaves into small cups.

ACTIVITY: Have the children brush glue over their bear shapes and place them in box lids. Then let the children sprinkle tea leaves on top of the glue and shake off the excess. Pour any leftover tea leaves back into the cups. Then let the children glue buttons or circle stickers on their bears for eyes and noses.

SENT IN BY: Joyce Marshall, Whitby, Ontario

VARIATION: Instead of tea leaves, use dried, leftover coffee grounds.

PEANUT BUTTER BEAR SANDWICHES

Whole-wheat bread slices   Raisins
Peanut butter   Maraschino cherries

Let the children use a heart-shaped cookie cutter to cut heart shapes out of bread slices (partially frozen bread cuts easily). Show them how to cut the points off their hearts to make the shapes resemble bear faces. Have the children spread peanut butter on their bear face shapes. Then let them use raisins to make eyes and mouths and cherries to make noses. (If desired, use unsweetened red berries instead of cherries.)

SENT IN BY: Nancy C. Windes, Denver, CO

FLANNELBOARD FUN

MATERIALS: A flannelboard; assorted colors of felt; pair of scissors.

PREPARATION: Cut a large mountain shape out of green felt. At the bottom, cut a flap to make a "door" (see illustration). Out of brown felt, cut two bear shapes, one that is standing and one that is curled up. Cut the curled-up bear to fit inside the "door" in the mountain. Decorate both bear shapes with small flowers cut from felt scraps. (Optional shapes to cut out: an airplane; a white blanket of snow to cover mountaintop; flowers for mountainside; people.)

ACTIVITY: Put the mountain shape on your flannelboard. Place the curled-up bear in the "door" opening and close the flap. Then read aloud *The Bear and the Mountain* and place the other felt shapes on the flannelboard to dramatize the action. (Just before the third to the last verse, remove the standing bear and open the flap in the mountain to reveal the curled-up bear.) When the children have become familiar with the story, let them take turns moving the shapes on the flannelboard.

Ellie the Evergreen

By Jean Warren

It was autumn. The trees in the park were busy changing into their new coats. Soon the park was filled with the colors of yellow, red, gold and brown.

All of the trees were excited and happy — all except Ellie. Ellie was an evergreen tree, and no matter how hard she wished, her needle coat remained green.

The people in town came to admire the beautiful coats on the other trees. The squirrels played in their colorful leaves. The children danced beneath their branches. Everyone said "Ooh!" and "Ahh!"

Ellie was sad. No one noticed her at all.

Soon the autumn days grew shorter, and the nights grew colder, and the winds began to blow. Soon the colorful leaves began to fly off the trees. One by one, the wind sent them twirling to the ground.

As the other trees lost their leaves, the people in town began to notice Ellie the Evergreen. The squirrels scampered in her warm branches. The children played beneath her outstretched arms when it rained. And when the first snows came, everyone admired her beauty.

One day the townspeople came to the park and placed colorful lights on Ellie's branches. When the lights were turned on, everyone smiled and said "Ooh!" and "Ahh!" There was no doubt about it — Ellie was now the most beautiful tree in the park!

Everyone was happy for Ellie, even the other trees. They knew that autumn was their season and that winter was Ellie's season.

Like the trees, we all have our season. All we have to do is wait.

Extended Activities
Ellie the Evergreen

LITTLE GREEN TREE
Sung to: "I'm a Little Teapot"

I'm a little green tree
By the house.
Here is my trunk,
  (Raise arms straight up.)
Here are my boughs.
  (Hold arms out to sides.)
Decorate me now with lights so fine,
  (Move hands back and forth across body.)
Then plug them in and watch me shine!
  (Hold arms out to sides and smile.)

Billie Taylor
Sioux City, IA

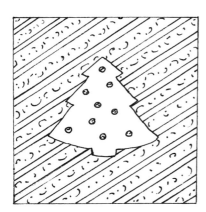

"LIGHTED" CHRISTMAS TREES

MATERIALS: An assortment of Christmas giftwrap; green construction paper; hole punch; pair of scissors; glue.

PREPARATION: For each child, cut a Christmas tree shape (about 4 inches tall) out of green construction paper. Cut Christmas giftwrap into 8-inch squares.

ACTIVITY: Let the children use a hole punch to punch holes in their Christmas tree shapes. (If necessary, fold trees in half vertically so holes can be punched in the center portions.) Then have the children "light up" their trees by moving their shapes around on top of squares of Christmas giftwrap and watching the various colors "shine" through the holes. When they have finished experimenting, let each child choose a square of giftwrap and glue his or her tree on it.

VARIATION: Instead of Christmas giftwrap, use brightly colored pictures cut from magazines.

YULE LOG SNACKS

Whole-wheat bread slices   Diced red and green peppers
Soft cream cheese

Let the children flatten slices of bread with a rolling pin. Have them spread cream cheese on their bread slices and sprinkle on red and green pepper pieces. Then have them roll up their bread slices to make "yule logs." (If desired, use deviled ham or peanut butter instead of cream cheese and omit the peppers.)

CHRISTMAS TREE DECORATING GAME

MATERIALS: A shoebox; assorted colors of felt; pair of scissors; glue; rickrack or yarn.

PREPARATION: Using green felt, cut out a Christmas tree shape (or a triangle shape) to fit inside the lid of the shoebox. Glue the tree inside the lid. Cut small circles out of other colors of felt for Christmas tree ornaments. Cut a star out of yellow felt for the top of the tree. Cut out small felt squares and rectangles for presents and glue on decorations of rickrack or yarn. Place all the loose shapes inside the shoebox.

GAME: Let the children take turns decorating the Christmas tree by placing on the felt ornaments and arranging the presents along the bottom edge of the tree. Ask the children to put the loose shapes back into the shoebox when their turns are over.

The Little Blue Dishes

Adapted by Elizabeth McKinnon

Long ago in Germany lived three children. Hans was the oldest. Peter came next. And Gretchen, who was just five, was their little sister.

On Christmas Eve, Hans went out to play, leaving Peter and Gretchen inside. It was almost Gretchen's bedtime, so Peter helped her to hang up her stocking.

"Do you know what you want for Christmas, Gretchen?" asked Peter.

"Oh, yes," said Gretchen. "What I want most of all is a set of little blue dishes!" Then she gave Peter a hug and went to bed.

Peter shook his money jar and out came one penny. He put the penny in his pocket and ran to the toy shop. "I want to buy a set of little blue dishes," he said to the shopkeeper. "I have one penny."

"The set of little blue dishes costs ten pennies," said the shopkeeper. "But you can buy this red candy heart for one penny."

So Peter bought the red candy heart, took it home and put it into Gretchen's stocking. Then he, too, went to bed.

Later, Hans came home. He reached into Gretchen's stocking and took out the candy heart. "Oh, this looks good!" he said. And in the wink of an eye, he ate it all up!

"Now I must buy something else for Gretchen," said Hans. He opened his money jar and counted out ten pennies. Then he took the money to the toy shop.

"What can I buy for ten pennies?" Hans asked.

"You can buy these little blue dishes," said the shopkeeper. "There is just one set left."

Hans gave the shopkeeper his ten pennies and ran home with the little blue dishes. He put them into Gretchen's stocking and then went to bed.

On Christmas morning Gretchen opened her stocking. How happy she was to find the set of little blue dishes! But Peter was very surprised. He didn't know how his red candy heart had turned into a set of little blue dishes overnight. Do you?

Author Unknown

Extended Activities
The Little Blue Dishes

CHRISTMASTIME IS HERE
Sung to: "The Farmer in the Dell"

Christmastime is here,
Christmastime is here.
Merry Christmas everyone!
Christmastime is here.

It's time to trim the tree,
It's time to trim the tree.
Merry Christmas everyone!
It's time to trim the tree.

It's time to wrap the gifts,
It's time to wrap the gifts.
Merry Christmas everyone!
It's time to wrap the gifts.

It's time to hang the stockings,
It's time to hang the stockings.
Merry Christmas everyone!
It's time to hang the stockings.

Additional verse: "Santa will soon be here."

Betty Ruth Baker
Waco, TX

LACED CHRISTMAS STOCKINGS

MATERIALS: Red tagboard; green yarn; hole punch; pair of scissors; tape.

PREPARATION: For each child, cut a stocking shape out of red tagboard. Use a hole punch to punch holes around the edge of each stocking. Cut green yarn into manageable lengths. Tape one end of a piece of yarn on the back of each stocking. Cover the other end with tape to make a "needle."

ACTIVITY: Let the children lace yarn through the holes in their stocking shapes. When they have finished, trim the remaining yarn ends and tape them to the backs of the stockings.

CRANBERRY GELATIN

1 cup fresh cranberries   1 packet unflavored gelatin
2 cups unsweetened apple juice

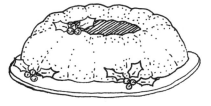

Put gelatin powder in a bowl. Heat 1 cup of the apple juice
and stir into gelatin. Place cranberries and remaining cup of
apple juice into a blender container and blend well. Pour the
mixture through a strainer. Discard pulp and add the cranapple
liquid to the gelatin mixture. Stir and pour into one large mold
or several small molds. Refrigerate until firm. (If desired, add
chopped nuts and fruits before refrigerating.)

Makes 8 small servings

CREATIVE DRAMATICS FUN

MATERIALS: (All optional) A large stocking; two baby food
jars with lids; eleven pennies; red and blue construction paper;
small index card; pair of scissors; glue.

PREPARATION: If desired, this activity can be done with
pretend props. Otherwise, put one penny into one baby food
jar and ten pennies into another jar. Cut a small heart shape
out of red construction paper. Cut a set of doll dishes out of
blue construction paper and glue the shapes on an index card.

ACTIVITY: Read *The Little Blue Dishes* aloud several times to
the children. When they have become familiar with the story,
let them take turns acting out the roles of the characters as you
read. Have the children use the props suggested above or let
them make appropriate movements to suggest props.

Eight Little Candles

By Jean Warren

Eight little candles, one by one,
Were waiting to join the holiday fun.

The first little candle standing in the row
Said, "Light me now so I can glow."

The second little candle, joining the plea,
Said, "Light me, too, so I can see."

The third little candle, wanting a turn,
Said, "Light me now so I can burn."

The fourth little candle standing in line
Said, "Light me, too, so I can shine."

The fifth little candle, hoping for the same,
Said, "I will dance if you light my flame."

The sixth little candle, standing so straight,
Said, "Light me now to celebrate."

The seventh little candle, so happy tonight,
Said, "It's my turn to get a light."

The eighth little candle, waiting so long,
Said, "I may be last, but my light is strong."

Now all eight candles are burning bright
Filling the world with the wonder of light.

Extended Activities
Eight Little Candles

EIGHT LITTLE CANDLES
Sung to: "Twinkle, Twinkle, Little Star"

Eight little candles in a row,
Waiting to join the holiday glow.
We will light them one by one
Until all eight have joined the fun.
Eight little candles burning bright,
Filling the world with holiday light.

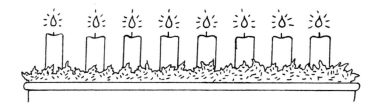

Jean Warren

CANDLE PUPPETS

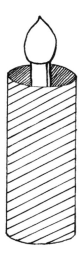

MATERIALS: Cardboard toilet tissue tubes; tempera paints; brushes; Popsicle sticks; yellow construction paper; pair of scissors; glue.

PREPARATION: For each child, cut a candle flame shape out of yellow construction paper.

ACTIVITY: Let the children paint their toilet tissue tubes any color they wish. Then have them each glue a precut candle flame shape on the end of a Popsicle stick. Show the children how to work their candle puppets by moving the Popsicle stick "flames" up and down inside the cardboard tube "candles."

VARIATION: Let the children press playdough into jar lids. Then have them anchor their painted cardboard tubes and Popsicle stick flames in the playdough to make stand-up candles.

CANDLE SALADS

Pineapple rings Carrot strips
Bananas Toothpicks
Lettuce leaves

For each salad, put a lettuce leaf on a plate and place a pineapple ring on top of the lettuce. Stand half of a peeled banana upright in the center of the pineapple ring. Cut off the pointed end of the banana. Use a potato peeler to peel off a strip of carrot. Roll the carrot strip into a ring, overlapping the ends. Stick one end of a toothpick through the ends of the carrot strip and one end down into the banana. Pinch the carrot ring to make it look like a pointed candle flame. (**Note:** Have the children remove the toothpicks before eating their salads.)

FLANNELBOARD FUN

MATERIALS: A flannelboard; assorted colors of felt; pair of scissors.

PREPARATION: For Hanukkah: Cut a menorah shape, nine candle shapes and nine yellow candle flame shapes out of felt.

ACTIVITY: Place the menorah with the nine candles standing in it on your flannelboard. Put a flame shape on top of the middle candle. Explain that with a real menorah, the candle in the middle would be used to light the other candles. Then read *Eight Little Candles* aloud and let the children take turns placing the candle flames on the eight remaining candles.

VARIATION: For Christmas: Cut eight candle shapes out of red felt and eight candle flame shapes out of yellow felt. (Decorate candles with holly leaf shapes cut from green felt, if desired.) Place the candles in a row on your flannelboard. Then read the story aloud and let the children take turns placing the candle flames on the eight candles.

Thousands of Valentines for Hundreds of Friends

By Susan M. Paprocki, Elmhurst, IL

Valentine's Day was not far away. The children in Bobby's class had some ideas about the kinds of valentines they were going to share with their friends.

"I'm passing out stickers!" Jill announced at circle time.

"My friends are going to get valentines with Popeye on them," Mike added.

Bobby sat very quietly. His teacher asked him if he had thought about valentines for his friends. Bobby smiled and explained that indeed he had big plans!

"I have *thousands* of valentines for *hundreds* of friends," said Bobby.

The other children looked at Bobby. He must be confused, or so they thought. No one has *hundreds* of friends. And how do you carry *thousands* of valentines? After all, the valentines were going to be placed in decorated shoeboxes. And thousands of valentines wouldn't fit in a shoebox.

Hundreds of friends? Thousands of valentines? IMPOSSIBLE!

Becky said that her hand began to hurt after signing just two valentines. How could Bobby be ready in time? The party was in two days.

"These valentines won't hurt my hand, and I'll have them ready in time," said Bobby, very sure of himself.

The next two days were busy ones. The children talked about caring, sharing and friendship. They cut out hearts and pasted them on their shoeboxes. They were very excited about filling their boxes with colorful valentines for their friends.

At last it was Valentine's Day. The children came to school with their decorated shoeboxes and placed them carefully on the table that their teacher had prepared.

Bobby placed his mysterious box on the table as well. The other children looked at it closely and decided it wasn't big enough to hold a thousand valentines. But Bobby reassured them that he had indeed kept his word.

When the party began, the children took turns passing out their valentines. Bobby's turn was last.

"Bobby," the other children insisted, "what about your valentines? Aren't you going to pass out your *thousands* of valentines to your *hundreds* of friends?"

"We have to go outside first," Bobby said.

The other children and the teacher were puzzled, but they put on their coats and hats and followed Bobby to the schoolyard. Once outside, they watched Bobby as he carefully uncovered his valentine box.

"It's filled with seeds...*thousands* of seeds!" shouted Becky.

"Why, those seeds are birdseed, children," the teacher explained.

"The birds are my special friends," said Bobby. "It's cold in February, and I can show my friends I care by giving them food during the cold winter."

Bobby let each child spread some birdseed on the ground. He kept the rest in his valentine box and placed it on the school windowsill.

Bobby's teacher smiled. "Your valentines are lovely, and your friends, the birds, will certainly enjoy your caring gift," she said.

Bobby was so pleased. He knew that he and the other children would enjoy watching the birds feast on his valentines for many weeks to come. And he had indeed shown that he had thousands of valentines for hundreds of friends. He cared and shared, and that is what Valentine's Day is all about.

Extended Activities
Thousands of Valentines for Hundreds of Friends

I'M A HAPPY LITTLE HEART
Sung to: "Little White Duck"

I'm a happy little heart
That's pink and white and red,
A happy little heart
With lace around my edge.
I have three words
On the front of me
That say "I love you,"
Oh, can't you see?
I'm a happy little heart
That's pink and white and red.
Happy little heart!

Gayle Bittinger

EASY "LACE" VALENTINES

MATERIALS: Red or pink construction paper; white gummed reinforcement circles; ballpoint pen or pencil.

PREPARATION: For each child, draw a large heart shape on a piece of red or pink construction paper. (Avoid using ink that runs when wet.)

ACTIVITY: Let the children lick and stick white reinforcement circles around the outlines of their heart shapes to create fancy, "lace-edged" valentines.

SENT IN BY: Betty Silkunas, Philadelphia, PA

VALENTINE SANDWICHES

White bread slices   Mayonnaise
Deviled ham   Alfalfa sprouts

Mix deviled ham with mayonnaise in a small bowl. Let the children use a heart-shaped cookie cutter to cut heart shapes out of bread slices. Then let them spread the pink deviled ham mixture on their heart shapes and sprinkle on alfalfa sprouts for a lacy touch.

VALENTINE PUZZLE PALS

MATERIALS: Red tagboard; pair of scissors.

PREPARATION: Cut large heart shapes (one for each pair of children) out of red tagboard. Cut each heart into two pieces to make a mini-puzzle. Cut each puzzle so that the pieces fit together differently.

GAME: Mix up the puzzle pieces and give one piece to each child. Then have the children move around the room and try to find their "valentine puzzle pals" by matching up their puzzle pieces. Since the last two children will be holding matching pieces, everyone will end up a winner. (If you have an uneven number of children, you or another adult can participate in the game.)

41

The Rabbit Who Ate the Snowman's Nose

By Marjorie Arneé, Pacific Grove, CA

Suzie Rabbit hopped slowly through the deep snow. She was tired and hungry, for she hadn't had a bite to eat since yesterday. Suzie had searched all over the neighborhood, looking for fresh green grass. But although it was the beginning of spring, a storm had hidden the grass under a deep covering of snow.

As she hopped into one yard, Suzie remembered the delicious tulip leaves that always grew in the flower bed. It was time for them to be up, and perhaps they would be growing above the snow. But when she reached the flower bed, she found that the snow had covered the tulip leaves, too.

Poor Suzie. Where could she find food under all the snow?

Like other rabbits, Suzie sometimes chewed on the bark of young trees if there was nothing else to eat. Suzie didn't like bark very much, but it was better than no food at all.

She hopped into the next yard where she knew that several young trees had just been planted. But again, she was disappointed. The people who lived in the house knew all about rabbits' eating habits, and they had wrapped the young tree trunks with heavy oiled cloth. There was no way Suzie could get to the bark underneath.

Suzie was so tired that her feet began to drag. And as she hopped away, she stumbled over a twig. She sat up, sneezing the snow from her whiskers. It was then that she spied the largest carrot she had ever seen. Some children had built a tall snowman that morning, and they had used the carrot for the snowman's nose.

Suzie jumped up and tried reaching for the carrot, but the snowman was too tall. She jumped and jumped as high as she could, but still she could not reach the carrot. She sat quietly for a moment, thinking.

Then she had an idea. She turned around and began to push the snow into a pile with her strong hind paws. Soon the snow pile was high enough for Suzie to stand on and reach the carrot. Quickly she hopped up on top of it.

But just as Suzie reached out for the snowman's nose, her kind heart made her stop.

"What will the snowman do without a nose?" she wondered. Then she decided, "I must find another nose for him."

When she looked out over the yard, Suzie spotted the twig that she had stumbled over. It looked about the right size. Suzie hopped down from the snow pile and picked up the twig.

"This will make a perfect nose for you, Mr. Snowman," she said. She hopped back up on the snow pile and took out the carrot. Then she placed the twig where the carrot nose had been.

Suzie Rabbit sat down on the snow pile and happily nibbled on her carrot. She had her dinner, and the snowman still had a nose.

Extended Activities
The Rabbit Who Ate the Snowman's Nose

THE SNOWMAN
Sung to: "The Muffin Man"

Have you seen the snowman,
The snowman, the snowman?
Have you seen the snowman
Who lives in our front yard?

He has two brown potato eyes,
Potato eyes, potato eyes.
He has two brown potato eyes
And lives in our front yard.

He has an orange carrot nose,
Carrot nose, carrot nose.
He has an orange carrot nose
And lives in our front yard.

He has a bright red berry smile,
Berry smile, berry smile.
He has a bright red berry smile
And lives in our front yard.

Additional verses: "He has a big, black top hat; He has a long, red woolen scarf."

Jean Warren

TORN-PAPER SNOWMEN

MATERIALS: Blue, white, black and orange construction paper; glue; pair of scissors; pencil.

PREPARATION: For each child, draw a large snowman shape on a piece of blue construction paper. Cut top hat shapes and stick shapes (for arms) out of black construction paper. Cut little triangles (for carrot noses) out of orange construction paper. Tear white and black construction paper into scraps for easy handling.

ACTIVITY: Have the children tear white paper scraps into little pieces and glue them on their snowmen until the entire shapes are filled. Let them glue orange triangle noses on their snowmen and add other facial features using tiny pieces torn from black paper scraps. Then let them glue on precut hats and arms.

SENT IN BY: Jane M. Spannbauer, So. St. Paul, MN

SNOWMAN SALADS

Cottage cheese　　　　Raisins
Lettuce leaves　　　　Small carrot sticks

Place lettuce leaves on plates and top with round scoops of cottage cheese. Then let the children make snowman faces on their scoops of cottage cheese, using raisins for eyes and mouths and carrot sticks for noses.

FIND THE SNOWMAN'S NOSE

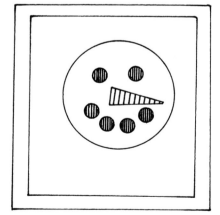

MATERIALS: A flannelboard; white, black and orange felt; pair of scissors.

PREPARATION: Cut a large circle out of white felt for a snowman face. Cut small circles out of black felt for eyes and a mouth, and a long triangle out of orange felt for a nose. Arrange the felt pieces on your flannelboard.

GAME: Have the children sit in a group by the flannelboard. Remove the snowman's orange nose and explain that you will be hiding it. Choose one child to be the Searcher and have the child close his or her eyes while you hide the nose. Then, as the child walks around the room searching for the nose, let the other children help by calling out "Hot!" if the Searcher is going in the right direction or "Cold!" if the Searcher is going in the wrong direction. When the Searcher finds the snowman's nose, have him or her place it back on the snowman's face. Then let another child have a turn being the Searcher.

45

The Brave Little Leprechaun

By Carolyn R. Simmons, Gothenburg, NE

Once upon a time, in a deep green forest in Ireland, lived a tiny little leprechaun by the name of Shawn.

Now everyone knows that leprechauns are small — very small, in fact. But Shawn was extra, extra small. Because he was so tiny, the other young leprechauns made fun of him and teased him. But Shawn didn't care. He was smart and brave, and he knew that he was just as good as the others.

Finally the day came for Shawn to leave home and seek his fortune. Like all young leprechauns, he had to go out and find his own pot of gold to bring back and hide in the forest.

Shawn's mother gave him a big kiss and wished him good luck. The other young leprechauns just laughed at tiny little Shawn. "Why, he couldn't carry a pot of gold even if he did find one!" they exclaimed.

Well, Shawn knew that he would find his pot of gold. After all, he was very clever, and being so small was an advantage. He could squeeze into tiny places and hide from the humans who were always out looking for leprechauns.

And so it was that one day, Shawn was hiding in a hollow log from a little boy he had spied running through the forest. Shawn was wondering why such a small boy would be out in the forest alone, when suddenly a low tree limb fell, trapping the little boy under its leafy branches.

Shawn could hear the little boy crying, but he didn't know what to do. His mother had warned him many times to beware of humans. But this one was so young, Shawn just had to help him.

Shawn crept out of his hiding place and peeked through the branches of the tree limb. The little boy wasn't hurt, but he was scared.

Shawn took hold of a branch and tugged with all his might. The tree limb was heavy, but tiny Shawn kept on tugging. Inch by inch, the tree limb began to move. And soon the little boy was able to crawl out from under it.

Just then, a large hand reached down and grabbed Shawn by the coattails. It was a human hand!

"Well, what have we here?" asked a big man.

Shawn tried to slip away. He knew that humans liked to catch leprechauns in hopes of getting their gold. He said, "I am a leprechaun, sir, but please let me go. I have no pot of gold to give you."

"Wait," said the man. "You did a brave thing just now. You risked getting caught to help my son. I don't want any gold from you. Instead, I want to give you a pot of gold for being so brave."

And so it was that Shawn returned home pulling a big pot of gold behind him. His mother gave him a hug and said how proud she was. And even though Shawn stayed just as tiny as ever, the other leprechauns never teased him or made fun of him again.

Extended Activities
The Brave Little Leprechaun

I'M A LITTLE LEPRECHAUN
Sung to: "I'm a Little Teapot"

I'm a little leprechaun
Dressed in green,
The tiniest man
That you ever have seen.
If you ever catch me, so it's told,
I'll give you my pot of gold!

Vicki Claybrook
Kennewick, WA

"LIVING" LEPRECHAUNS

MATERIALS: Styrofoam cups; dirt or potting soil; alfalfa seeds; green construction paper; cotton balls; pair of scissors; glue; water.

PREPARATION: Cut eye and mouth shapes out of green construction paper.

ACTIVITY: Have the children make leprechaun faces on the sides of their Styrofoam cups by gluing on precut facial features and cotton ball "beards." When the glue has dried, let the children fill their cups with dirt or potting soil and sprinkle on alfalfa seeds and water. Place the leprechaun cups in a sunny spot and have the children water them each day. Alfalfa seeds sprout quickly, and it won't be long before each leprechaun has a head of green "hair."

LEPRECHAUN LUNCH

Lettuce leaves   Salad dressing
Green vegetables (celery,
cucumbers, peas, green peppers,
avacados, sprouts, etc.)

Let the children wash and dry the lettuce leaves, tear them into pieces and put them in a salad bowl. Cut up the other green vegetables and add them to the lettuce. Then pour on the salad dressing and let the children help toss the salad before serving. (Try adding a few drops of green food coloring to the salad dressing, if desired.)

LEPRECHAUN'S GOLD

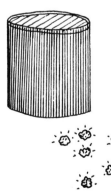

MATERIALS: A coffee can; one die; gold foil or yellow construction paper; black construction paper; pair of scissors; tape.

PREPARATION: Tape black construction paper around a coffee can to make a "pot of gold." Make "gold pieces" by crumpling small squares of gold foil into balls or by cutting circles out of yellow construction paper. Put the foil balls or yellow circles into the coffee can.

GAME: Choose one child to be the Leprechaun and have him or her sit in a chair, holding the "pot of gold." Let each child in turn walk up to the Leprechaun and ask, "Leprechaun, will you give me some gold?" Have the Leprechaun reply, "Yes, I will when a number I'm told." Have the child roll the die and name the number that comes up on it. Then have the Leprechaun give the child that number of "gold pieces." Continue the game until everyone has had a turn. Then choose one of the children who rolled a high number to be the next Leprechaun.

Buzzy Bee's Rainy Day

By Donna Mullennix, Thousand Oaks, CA

Buzzy Bee was a hard worker. Every day he flew among the flowers, buzzing and singing,

> "I'm a buzzy little bee,
> I'm busy as can be.
> I buzz to the flowers,
> One — two — three."

Buzzy flew on sunny days and on cloudy days. He buzzed on windy days and on still days. The only time he stopped buzzing was when it rained. On rainy days Buzzy Bee stayed inside the hive to keep dry.

One spring it rained and rained and rained. Buzzy Bee stayed inside his hive for five days. Then he said, "Bzzz. I'm tired of staying inside. I think I'll go out and buzz in the rain."

Buzzy had never been in the rain before. He flew out of the hive singing,

> "I'm a buzzy little bee,
> I'm busy as can be.
> I buzz to the flowers,
> One — two — three."

When he reached the garden, Buzzy was surprised to see that the flowers had shut their petals tight and were sleeping in the rain. "Wake up! Wake up!" he cried. But the flowers didn't hear him. So Buzzy decided to buzz around and see what else there was in the spring world besides flowers.

When he looked down, Buzzy saw a snail crawling slowly through the garden. "I love it when it rains," said the snail. "It's my favorite kind of weather. I love to crawl under the wet leaves and look for things to eat."

"Not me," said Buzzy. "I want it to stop raining so the flowers will wake up, for

> I'm a buzzy little bee,
> I'm busy as can be.
> I buzz to the flowers,
> One — two — three."

Away flew Buzzy to a pond where he saw a frog hopping and croaking beside the water. "I love it when it rains," said the frog. "It's my favorite kind of weather. I love to get wet and hop in the mud."

"Not me," said Buzzy. "I want it to stop raining so the flowers will wake up, for

> I'm a buzzy little bee,
> I'm busy as can be.
> I buzz to the flowers,
> One — two — three."

Buzzy flew out to the middle of the pond where he saw a duck swimming and quacking in the water. "I love it when it rains," said the duck. "It's my favorite kind of weather. I love to swim and feel the rain running off my feathers."

"Not me," said Buzzy. "I want it to stop raining so the flowers will wake up, for

> I'm a buzzy little bee,
> I'm busy as can be.
> I buzz to the flowers,
> One — two — three."

Buzzy suddenly felt something warm on his back. He looked up into a clear sky. The rain had stopped, and now the sun was shining. "Bzzz," said Buzzy. "I love it when the sun shines. It's *my* favorite kind of weather!"

He flew back to the garden where the flowers were just waking up. When they saw Buzzy, they smiled and nodded their heads at him. Buzzy flapped his little wings and sang,

> "I'm a HAPPY little bee,
> I'm busy as can be.
> I buzz to the flowers,
> One — two — three!"

Extended Activities
Buzzy Bee's Rainy Day

BUMBLEBEE ON MY NOSE
Sung to: "Jingle Bells"

Bumblebee, bumblebee,
Landing on my toes.
Bumblebee, bumblebee,
Now he's on my nose.
On my arms, on my legs,
On my elbows.
Bumblebee, oh, bumblebee,
He lands and then he goes!

Have the children touch their toes, noses, etc. as they
sing the song. Then repeat, substituting the name "Buzzy
Bee" for "bumblebee."

Jean Warren

BALLOON BEES

MATERIALS: Yellow balloons; black felt-tip markers; circle
stickers (optional).

PREPARATION: Blow up the balloons.

ACTIVITY: Let the children create "bees" by drawing stripes
around their yellow balloons with black felt-tip markers. If
desired, have them attach circle stickers for eyes (or have them
draw eyes on their bees with the markers). When the children
have finished, let them toss their balloon bees up and down in
the air and "buzz" around the room.

SENT IN BY: Betty Silkunas, Philadelphia, PA

A TASTE OF HONEY

Honey   Sesame seeds
Carrot sticks

Put small amounts of honey into paper cups and add sesame seeds. Then let the children dip carrot sticks into the honey for a sweet "bee snack." (If desired, use apple slices or orange segments instead of carrot sticks.)

MUSICAL BEES

MATERIALS: A chair for each child; music; construction paper; crayons or felt-tip markers; tape.

PREPARATION: Have the children each draw a picture of a flower on a piece of construction paper. Tape one picture on each chair and place the chairs back-to-back in a double line. Set up music, if necessary.

GAME: Ask the children to pretend that they are bees and that the chairs are flowers. Start the music and have the children "buzz" around the line of chairs. When you stop the music, have each child sit down on the chair by which he or she is standing. Continue the game as long as interest lasts.

SENT IN BY: Colraine Pettipaw Hunley, Doylestown, PA

The Colorful Easter Eggs

By Carol McMichael, Indianapolis, IN

It was almost Easter. Mr. Rabbit sat impatiently inside his cozy burrow, looking out at the snow that had fallen the night before.

"How will I ever be able to decorate my special eggs and hide them in time for the Easter Egg Hunt?" he wondered. "The store has run out of the colors I need, and now — all this snow! Oh my whiskers! Oh my whiskers! What shall I do?"

Mrs. Rabbit sat in her rocking chair, busily knitting. "Don't worry, dear," she said comfortingly. "It snows *every* year at Eastertime, and *every* year the storekeeper runs out of the colors you use for your special eggs. But things always turn out just fine. Look, I've almost finished knitting your sweater to wear for Easter."

The next morning Mr. Rabbit scampered to the window to see if the snow had melted. But not only was the snow still there, it looked even deeper than before.

"Oh my whiskers! Oh my whiskers! What shall I do?" he worried. "Tomorrow is Easter, and I can't decorate my eggs because I have no colors. I can't hide white eggs — the children would never find them in all this white snow."

"Don't worry, dear," said Mrs. Rabbit. "Things will turn out just fine. Look, I've finished knitting your new sweater. Why don't you try it on while you're thinking about how you will decorate your eggs?"

As Mr. Rabbit pulled the sweater over his head, it occurred to him — THE SWEATER! YARN! OF COURSE!

"Oh my whiskers! Oh my whiskers! Now I know what to do!" exclaimed Mr. Rabbit. "Dear wife, would you please help me knit colored yarn around my eggs?"

"Why certainly," said Mrs. Rabbit. "What a good idea!" And they set to work immediately, knitting beautiful, colored yarn around each egg.

All day and all night they worked. They knitted some eggs in bright blue yarn, some in bright red and some in sunny yellow. They knitted some eggs in deep purple and others in yarn that was all the colors of the rainbow. By Easter morning each egg was decorated in its own way with brightly colored yarn.

"Oh my whiskers! Oh my whiskers! It's done! It's finished!" Mr. Rabbit cried happily. "Thanks to you, dear wife, I was able to decorate my eggs in time for the Easter Egg Hunt. Now the children will be able to find my eggs when I hide them in the snow."

Mr. Rabbit put the brightly colored eggs in a basket and started out the door.

"I told you not to worry, dear," said Mrs. Rabbit. "I knew everything would turn out just fine."

Extended Activities
The Colorful Easter Eggs

THE BUNNY PATCH
Sung to: "The Pawpaw Patch"

Let's go look for Easter eggs,
Let's go look for Easter eggs,
Let's go look for Easter eggs,
Way down yonder in the Bunny Patch.

Picking up eggs, put 'em in my basket,
Picking up eggs, put 'em in my basket,
Picking up eggs, put 'em in my basket,
Way down yonder in the Bunny Patch.

Little red eggs, in my basket,
Little blue eggs, in my basket,
Little green eggs, in my basket,
Way down yonder in the Bunny Patch.

Jean Warren

YARN-COVERED EGGS

MATERIALS: White Styrofoam meat trays or white cardboard; assorted colors of yarn; pair of scissors; tape.

PREPARATION: For each child, cut an egg shape out of a white Styrofoam meat tray or a white sheet of cardboard. Cut slits around the edges of the egg shapes. Cut yarn into manageable lengths. Tape one end of a piece of yarn to the back of each egg shape and pull it through one of the slits.

ACTIVITY: Let the children wind yarn around their egg shapes, each time passing the yarn through one of the slits. Encourage them to crisscross their egg shapes in any way they wish to create designs. When the children have finished, trim off the ends of the yarn and tape them to the backs of the egg shapes.

PEAR BUNNIES

Pear halves
Cottage cheese
Lettuce leaves

Whole cloves
Almond halves

For each serving, put a lettuce leaf on a plate and place a pear half (flat side down) on top of the lettuce. At the narrow end of the pear, insert two whole cloves for eyes and two almond halves for ears. At the other end of the pear, place a spoonful of cottage cheese for a fluffy white tail. (**Note:** Have the children remove the cloves before eating their pear bunnies.)

EASTER EGG HUNT

MATERIALS: Paper lunch sacks; assorted colors of construction paper or wallpaper samples; pair of scissors; glue or stapler.

PREPARATION: Cut the lunch sacks in half and use the bottom halves to make baskets. For each basket, cut a handle out of a different colored piece of construction paper or wallpaper and glue or staple it to the sides of the sack. Then cut six small egg shapes for each basket from paper that matches the handle. Hide the eggs in various places around the room.

GAME: Give the children each a basket and let them go on an Easter Egg Hunt. When they find eggs that match their handles, have them put the eggs in their baskets. Continue the game until all the eggs have been found.

SENT IN BY: Judith Hanson, Newton Falls, OH

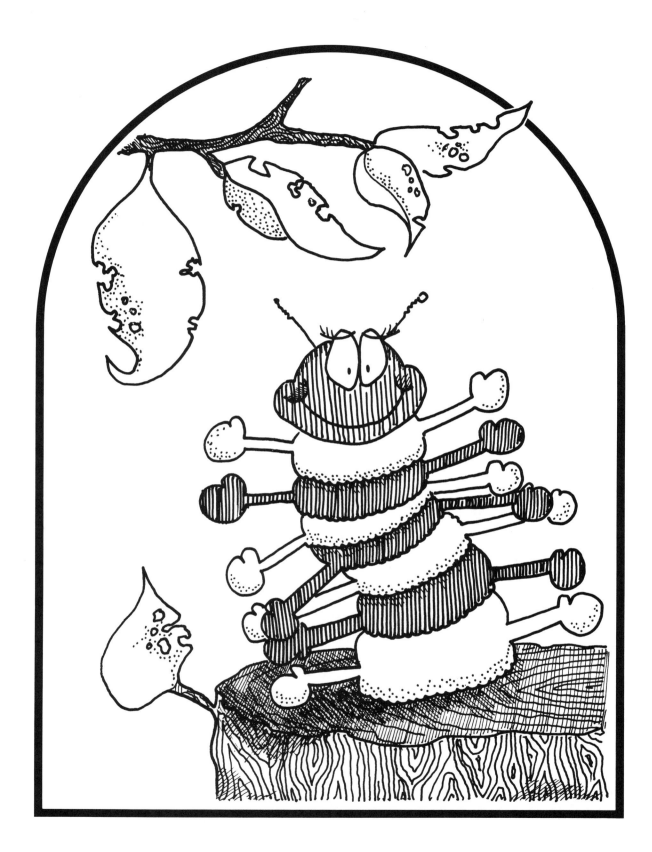

Katie the Caterpillar

By Jean Warren

Once upon a time there was a fuzzy little caterpillar named Katie.

Katie liked visiting new places. But she crawled so slowly that it took her a long time to get anywhere.

One day Katie crawled up on a shiny red bike. She had a marvelous time as a boy rode the bike around and around the block.

Katie liked going fast. But she wanted to go even faster. So she crawled down to the train yard and climbed aboard a train.

Katie traveled far across the country. Faster and faster went the train. Faster and faster went Katie.

At last Katie got off the train. "I want to go really fast," she said. "I want to fly." So she crawled over to the airport and climbed aboard a jet plane.

Katie held on with all her might as the plane flew higher and higher. Faster and faster went Katie, back across the country.

Katie loved flying. She didn't want the ride to end. But finally the plane landed, and Katie got off.

Suddenly Katie felt very tired. She crawled home to her favorite tree and curled up on a leaf. Then she spun a soft little blanket around herself and fell asleep.

Katie dreamed about flying. She loved it so much that she wished she could fly forever.

When Katie woke up, she felt strange. She wiggled out of her little blanket. Then she discovered that while she was sleeping, she had grown a pair of beautiful wings!

Now Katie was a butterfly, and she could fly forever! Now she knew that some wishes really do come true.

Extended Activities
Katie the Caterpillar

THE FUZZY CATERPILLAR
Sung to: "Eensy Weensy Spider"

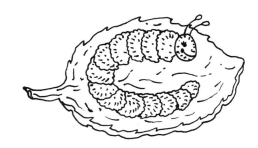

The fuzzy caterpillar
Curled up upon a leaf,
Spun her little chrysalis
And then fell fast asleep.
While she was sleeping,
She dreamed that she could fly.
And later when she woke up,
She was a butterfly!

Elizabeth McKinnon

EGG CARTON CATERPILLARS

MATERIALS: Cardboard egg cartons; pipe cleaners; pair of scissors; crayons or tempera paints and brushes.

PREPARATION: Remove egg carton lids and save them for other uses. Cut each egg carton in half lengthwise.

ACTIVITY: Give each of the children an egg carton half to use as a caterpillar body. Help each child poke the point of a folded pipe cleaner into the top of one end section to make "feelers." Then let the children use crayons or paints to make eyes and designs on their caterpillars.

SENT IN BY: Cathy Phillips, Clarkston, MI

VARIATION: Use Styrofoam egg cartons and let the children paint them with a mixture of dry tempera and liquid soap.

MELON BALL CATERPILLARS

Melon balls   Lettuce leaves
Whole cloves   Toothpicks

To make each caterpillar, thread three melon balls on a king-sized toothpick (or use ordinary toothpicks to fasten the melon balls together in a row). In one of the end melon balls, partially insert two whole cloves for "feelers." Serve each melon ball caterpillar on a lettuce leaf. (**Note:** Have the children remove the cloves and the toothpicks before eating their melon ball caterpillars.)

CATERPILLAR WALK

MATERIALS: None.

PREPARATION: None.

ACTIVITY: Have the children form a "caterpillar" by lining up in a row on their knees. Ask each child to hold onto the back or the legs of the person in front of him or her. Then have the children crawl together in a line by taking steps first with their right knees, then with their left knees, etc. Sing the song below as the children take their "caterpillar walk."

Sung to: "Frere Jacques"

Caterpillar, caterpillar,
Crawl, crawl, crawl; crawl, crawl, crawl.
Crawling on the ground,
Crawling all around.
Crawl, crawl, crawl; crawl, crawl, crawl.

Continue the activity as long as interest lasts.

Daddy Duck's Surprises

By Donna Mullennix, Thousand Oaks, CA

Daddy Duck was looking for his eggs. They were special eggs because they had surprises inside. He waddled through the field, quacking and looking.

Nearby, Daddy Duck heard a quiet sound. "Ssss-ssss." It was a beautiful black snake. "Quack," said Daddy Duck. "Have you seen my eggs? They have surprises inside."

"No," hissed Mother Snake. "But let me show you my egg. It has a surprise inside, too, and here it comes!" Mother Snake's egg was hatching, and out came one baby black snake.

"What a nice baby snake," said Daddy Duck. "But I must find *my* eggs with the surprises inside." And away he waddled, quacking and looking.

Soon Daddy Duck came to a tree where he heard a "tweet-tweet" high above him. "Quack!" he shouted. "Have you seen my eggs? They have surprises inside."

Mother Bird looked down and chirped, "No, but I have two eggs here in my nest. They have surprises inside, too, and here they come!" Mother Bird's eggs were hatching, and out came two baby birds. They peeked over the nest at Daddy Duck.

"Those are fine baby birds," said Daddy Duck. "But I must find *my* eggs with the surprises inside." And away he waddled, quacking and looking.

When Daddy Duck waddled by the hen house, he heard a "cluck-cluck" from inside. "Quack," he said as he looked in the door. "Have you seen my eggs? They have surprises inside."

"No," clucked Mother Hen. "But let me show you my three eggs. They have surprises inside, too, and here they come!" Mother Hen's eggs were hatching, and out came three baby chicks. They peeped at Daddy Duck.

"What beautiful baby chicks," said Daddy Duck. "But I must find *my* eggs with the surprises inside." And away he waddled, quacking and looking.

Soon Daddy Duck came to a pond. "Ribbit-ribbit," said Mother Frog. "Quack," said Daddy Duck. "Have you seen my eggs? They have surprises inside."

"I haven't seen them," croaked Mother Frog. "But let me show you my four eggs. They have surprises inside, too, and here they come!" On a leaf in the pond, Mother Frog's eggs were hatching, and out swam four tadpoles.

"What wonderful baby tadpoles," said Daddy Duck. "But I must keep looking for *my* eggs with the surprises inside." And away he waddled, quacking and looking.

Then Daddy Duck heard a familiar sound — "Quack-quack." Just ahead, in a tall clump of grass, was Mother Duck.

"Oh, Mother Duck," said Daddy Duck, "I'm so glad I found you. I have been looking and looking for our eggs. I found one snake egg, two bird eggs, three chicken eggs and four frog eggs — all with wonderful surprises inside. But I can't find our eggs. Do you know where they are?"

"Quack," whispered Mother Duck as she stepped out of the grass. "I have been sitting on our five eggs to keep them warm, and look what is happening!" Mother and Daddy Duck's eggs were hatching, and out came five little ducklings. "Peep, peep, peep, peep, peep!" they said.

Mother and Daddy Duck were very proud and very happy. They wanted to show their wonderful surprises to the snakes, the birds, the chickens and the frogs. So off waddled Mother and Daddy Duck and their five ducklings, quacking and peeping all the way.

Extended Activities
Daddy Duck's Surprises

HATCHING EGGS
Sung to: "Row, Row, Row Your Boat"

Eggs, eggs, hatching now,
Hatching one by one.
"Quack, quack," says Mother Duck,
"Here my ducklings come!"

Eggs, eggs, hatching now,
Hatching one by one.
"Croak, croak," says Mother Frog,
"Here my tadpoles come!"

Eggs, eggs, hatching now,
Hatching one by one.
"Cluck, cluck," says Mother Hen,
"Here my baby chicks come!"

Eggs, eggs, hatching now,
Hatching one by one.
"Tweet, tweet," says Mother Bird,
"Here my baby birds come!"

Additional verse: " 'Hiss, hiss,' says Mother Snake/'Here my baby snakes come!' "

Elizabeth McKinnon

FEATHERY DUCKS

MATERIALS: Yellow construction paper; yellow feathers (available at craft stores); pair of scissors; brushes; glue.

PREPARATION: For each child, cut a duck shape out of yellow construction paper.

ACTIVITY: Have the children brush glue over their duck shapes. Then let them stick feathers on the glue.

VARIATIONS: Let the children glue brown feathers on bird shapes or white feathers on chicken shapes.

BIRD NEST SALADS

Grated carrots   Mayonnaise
Canned chow mein noodles   Grapes or peas

Cut carrots in half and let the children help grate them. For each serving, mix together one half of a grated carrot and 1/4 cup chow mein noodles. Stir in mayonnaise to moisten. Place mixture on a plate and push the back of a spoon down into the middle to form a "nest." Let the children place grapes or peas in their nests for "eggs." (If desired, serve nests on top of lettuce leaves.)

BABY DUCKS

MATERIALS: None.

PREPARATION: None.

GAME: Have the children sit in a group. Choose one child to be the Mother (or Father) Duck and have the child leave the room. Choose two or three other children to be the Baby Ducks and have all the children lower their heads and cover their mouths with their hands. Have the Mother Duck return and walk around the group saying "Quack, quack." As she does so, have the Baby Ducks make peeping sounds. When the Mother Duck thinks that a child is one of her ducklings, have her tap the child on the shoulder. If the Mother Duck guesses correctly, have the Baby Duck raise his or her head. When the Mother Duck has found all of her babies, select new players and start the game again.

VARIATIONS: Follow the same procedure to play Baby Frogs, Baby Chicks, Baby Birds or Baby Snakes.

Dandy

By Jean Warren

Baby Dandy was excited. His tiny seed body was ripe, and his white, feathery parachute had just opened. Soon he would be separating from his family and venturing out on his own.

Dandy's parent plant was gradually letting go. When free, Dandy would be able to catch a ride on a friendly breeze and sail out to see the world. Like most dandelion seeds, Dandy planned to travel a bit before settling down in a safe place where he could grow into a plant himself.

At last it was time to go. Dandy waved goodbye to his family and hopped aboard a strong breeze. Up over the treetops he flew. The view was wonderful! Dandy never imagined that there could be so many different places to see. How would he ever be able to choose a place to land?

Soon Dandy spotted a big green field that looked perfect. Geronimo! Dandy jumped off the breeze and started to parachute down. But before he reached the ground, an angry wind snatched Dandy up, tossed him around and carried him far out over the ocean.

As the wind died down, Dandy began to fall. "Oh, no!" he cried. "If I land in the water, I'll never be able to grow into a plant!"

Down, down Dandy fell. But before he reached the water, a gentle breeze picked him up and carried him back over the land.

Before long Dandy spied a garden in back of a small house. "That's the place for me," he said. He thanked the gentle breeze for the ride, and off he jumped.

Down Dandy fell toward the garden, straight down to — oh, no! — the *dog* in the garden! Dandy landed right on top of the dog's back!

Around and around the garden went the dog. Around and around the garden went Dandy.

At last the dog stopped and gave himself a good shake. Dandy flew off the dog's back. But before he reached the ground, a fast wind swept him up and carried him out over a shopping mall.

As the wind died this time, Dandy went floating down toward the parking lot. "Oh, no!" he cried. "If I land on the pavement, I'll never be able to grow into a plant!"

Down, down Dandy fell — down, down into the back end of a truck that was filled with hay. Soon the truck began to move, and off went the load of hay with Dandy riding on top of it.

When the truck stopped by a gate, two men got out and began tossing the hay to the ground. Off Dandy flew and landed on the cap of a little girl who was standing nearby.

"Oh, no!" cried Dandy. "Will I never find a safe place to land?"

As the truck drove away, the little girl took off her cap and waved to the two men.

Down fell Dandy, down to the ground by the gate. At last he had landed in a safe place! At last he could burrow deep into the soil and send out his roots.

Before long Dandy began to grow up straight and tall. Soon he was a full-grown dandelion. And when the little girl left for school and came home each day, Dandy was there by the gate to greet her with his sunny yellow smile.

Extended Activities
Dandy

DANDY LADY
Sung to: "Mary Had a Little Lamb"

Little Dandy Lady,
Lady, Lady,
Little Dandy Lady
Was quite vain, they say.

She had hair of yellow,
Yellow, yellow.
She had hair of yellow
And loved to dance all day.

As she grew older,
Older, older,
As she grew older,
Her hair all turned to gray.

Now when she dances,
Dances, dances,
Now when she dances,
Her hair all blows away!

Repeat, substituting the word "dandelion" for "Dandy Lady" and changing "she/her" to "he/his."

Jean Warren

SPONGE-PRINT DANDELIONS

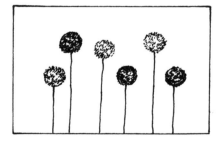

MATERIALS: Light blue construction paper; sponges; thick yellow tempera paint; thin white tempera paint; green crayons; pair of scissors; paper towels; shallow containers.

PREPARATION: Cut sponges into circle shapes. Place folded paper towels in shallow containers and pour on tempera paints. Use a green crayon to draw "stems" on sheets of light blue construction paper. Make one sheet for each child.

ACTIVITY: Let the children dip circle sponge shapes into yellow and white paint. Then have them press the shapes on their papers at the tops of the "stems" to create "dandelions." Let the children use green crayons to add leaves, if they wish.

DANDELION EGGS

Dandelion greens   Milk
Eggs   Margarine

Let the children help pick and wash some young, tender dandelion greens. Have them pat the greens dry with paper towels and tear them into little pieces. Mix eggs with milk and scramble them in melted margarine. Just before the eggs become firm, add the dandelion greens. Continue cooking until the eggs are done. (If desired, sprinkle on grated Cheddar cheese when adding the greens.)

DANDELION FUN

MATERIALS: Dandelions; water.

PREPARATION: None.

ACTIVITY: Take the children on a nature walk to pick dandelions. Then show them how to do one or more of the following:

—Use your thumbnail to slit the sides of dandelion stems down to the cut-off ends. Dip the stems in water to make "curls" and wear them tucked over your ears.

—Hold a dandelion in your fist and use your thumb to flip off the flower head. (Save the flowers to make a "floating garden" in a bowl of water, if desired.)

—Start a dandelion chain by making a slit in the stem of one dandelion and pulling the stem of another dandelion through the slit. Continue the process until you have a long chain.

—Blow seeds from dandelion tops by saying words that begin with the "wh" sound ("which, why, whisper," etc.).

Encourage the children to think of other fun things they can do with their dandelions.

I Hate Tomatoes

By Marjorie Kaufman, Stony Brook, NY

It was our first spring in our very first house. Mom and I decided to plant a vegetable garden.

So we went to a nursery. On the way I kept thinking, "Why are we going to a *school* to get plants?" But it wasn't a nursery for children. It was a plant nursery. That's a place where different kinds of vegetables, fruits and flowers are grown. You can buy the plants and then take them home to grow in your own garden.

We bought some zucchini plants — zucchini is my favorite vegetable — and then we bought some tomato plants.

I told Mom, "I hate tomatoes."

"Josh," she said, "you shouldn't hate anything because there's some good in everything."

"I know, but I *still* hate tomatoes!" I said.

After we got home we cleared away some grass along the sunny side of the house. Then we dug up the dirt to make a garden. We made holes in the dirt and put the little plants we had bought inside them. We covered up the roots with dirt and watered the plants with the hose. Then we put wire cages around the tomato plants so they would grow straight and tall and so the rabbits and the squirrels wouldn't eat them.

Mom and I were happy when our garden was planted, and we both smiled as we washed our hands.

In just a few weeks the tomato plants had grown tall. I kept telling Mom that I hated tomatoes. But Mom kept telling me I didn't and that she would prove it.

"Josh, what's your favorite food?" she asked.

"Pizza," I replied.

"Well, wait until we grow our first tomatoes. We'll make a pizza you'll never forget!" she assured me.

I didn't know what she meant.

I waited and waited. I watered and watered. Soon little yellow flowers began blooming on the tomato plants.

I waited and waited. I watered and watered. The little yellow flowers changed into tiny green tomatoes. They grew and grew.

By the end of summer the tomato plants had grown as tall as the wire cages, and the tomatoes were changing from green to orange. When they finally changed to red, Mom said they were ripe.

I got to pick the first red tomatoes. They were smooth and sweet smelling. I left them on the kitchen windowsill, and they grew even redder.

Finally it was time to make our pizza. We cut up the tomatoes and cooked them in a pan on top of the stove. As the tomatoes cooked, they turned into tomato sauce. Then we made dough out of flour and water in a big mixing bowl. We flattened the dough and rolled it into a circle with a rolling pin. Then we put on the tomato sauce with a big spoon, and on top of that we put a special kind of cheese called mozzarella.

We put our finished pizza on a flat pan and baked it in the oven. When it was done, we took it out and let it cool for awhile. Then I tasted it. It was the BEST!

Mom was right. I say I hate tomatoes. But I guess I don't really hate them after all!

Extended Activities
I Hate Tomatoes

THE TOMATO SONG
Sung to: "Little White Duck"

I'm a little green tomato
Growing on the vine,
A little green tomato
Looking oh, so fine.
The sun and rain, they help me so,
I'll get redder as I grow and grow.
I'm a little green tomato
Growing on the vine.
Grow, grow, grow.

I'm a big red tomato
Growing on the vine,
A big red tomato
Looking oh, so fine.
Now you can make good things with me —
Soup, juice, pizza, to name just three.
I'm a big red tomato
Growing on the vine.
Grow, grow, grow.

Sing the first verse in a tiny, high voice and the second verse in a big, deep voice.

Jean Warren

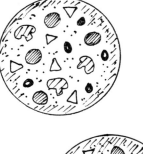

COLLAGE PIZZAS

MATERIALS: Cardboard pizza wheels or sheets of cardboard; dry red tempera paint; liquid starch; assorted colors of construction paper; yellow cornmeal; salt shaker or spice bottle with perforated lid; pair of scissors; large brushes; paint containers.

PREPARATION: If not using pizza wheels, cut a circle out of cardboard for each child. Put yellow cornmeal in a shaker container. Cut various kinds of pizza topping shapes out of colored construction paper (brown pepperoni circles, black olive slices, yellow pineapple wedges, tan mushroom slices, etc.). Mix dry red tempera with liquid starch and pour into paint containers.

ACTIVITY: Have the children brush red paint "tomato sauce" generously over their pizza wheels or cardboard circles. Then let them arrange precut "pizza toppings" on top of the wet paint and sprinkle on yellow cornmeal "cheese."

SENT IN BY: Ruth Engle, Kirkland, WA

MINI-PIZZAS

English muffin halves   Grated cheese
Pizza sauce

Brown the English muffin halves under a broiler. Then let the children spread pizza sauce on their muffin halves and sprinkle cheese on top of the sauce. Put the muffin halves back under the broiler until the cheese is hot and bubbly. Let cool before serving. (If desired, let the children add other toppings such as pepperoni slices, chopped green peppers, sliced olives, etc.)

TOMATO PLANTING GAME

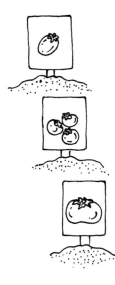

MATERIALS: A large sandbox; seed catalog; small index cards; tongue depressors; pair of scissors; glue.

PREPARATION: Cut 12 pictures of tomato plants from a seed catalog and glue the pictures on index cards (supplement with hand-drawn pictures, if necessary). Glue the index cards on tongue depressors to make "tomato plants."

GAME: Let the children "plant the tomatoes" in the sandbox as you give directions. For example, ask them to plant the tomatoes in two straight rows; in three straight rows; in four straight rows. (Encourage them to plant the rows from back to front and from left to right.) Or ask them to plant two tomatoes in the middle of the box; three tomatoes in a corner of the box; four tomatoes along the left-hand side of the box; a big tomato next to a little tomato, etc. Then let the children experiment with planting the tomatoes in ways they think up themselves.

The Tale of the Old Cactus

By Jean Warren

Way out on the desert
That's covered with sand,
Lives a big old cactus
Who's really quite grand.

He lives all alone
Beside the old trail.
And if you just ask him,
He'll tell you this tale.

When he was a young boy,
He always played rough.
But he never was hurt,
For a cactus is tough.

But then one night
When he went to bed,
He felt a small bump
On the side of his head.

Now during the night
The little bump grew,
And the cactus got worried.
Oh, what should he do?

He called to the doctor,
And the doctor said,
"Don't worry, young lad,
It's all in your head!"

He called to his granddad
Who lived on the range.
"Don't worry," said Granddad,
"We all must change."

But he was still worried.
Oh, what could it be?
The bump on his head
Was strange to see.

And then one day,
Before he knew,
Out of his bump
A flower grew!

Now the cactus is happy,
For this he does know —
We all must change
Before we can grow.

So if in the desert
The cactus you spy,
Look for his family
As you're passing by.

Each cactus is growing
And changing each day.
And so are you
In your special way!

**Adapted from *Carlos Discovers Change*
by Katherine I. Skiff**

Extended Activities
The Tale of the Old Cactus

THE TALE OF THE OLD CACTUS
Sung to: "On Top of Old Smokey"

Way out on the desert
That's covered with sand,
Lives a big old cactus
Who's really quite grand.

He lives all alone
Beside the old trail.
And if you just ask him,
He'll tell you this tale.

When he was a young boy,
He always played rough.
But he never was hurt,
For a cactus is tough.

But then one night
When he went to bed,
He felt a small bump
On the side of his head.

Continue singing additional verses from the story on p. 75.

Jean Warren

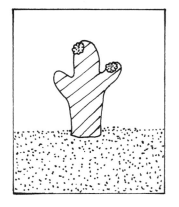

DESERT SCENES

MATERIALS: Light blue construction paper; sand; green construction paper; straw flowers or colored construction paper scraps; pair of scissors; brushes; glue.

PREPARATION: For each child, cut a cactus shape out of green construction paper. If not using straw flowers, cut small flower shapes out of brightly colored construction paper scraps.

ACTIVITY: Have the children brush glue across the bottom of light blue construction paper and sprinkle sand on the glue. When their papers have dried, let them glue on precut cactus shapes. Then have them glue straw flowers or precut flower shapes on their cactus shapes to complete their desert scenes.

VARIATION: Instead of flowers, let the children glue pieces of broken toothpicks on their cactus shapes for "spines."

DESERT THIRST QUENCHERS

Club soda   Ice cubes
Unsweetened fruit juice

Put ice cubes into plastic glasses. Then pour equal amounts of club soda and fruit juice over the ice to make cool, refreshing drinks for a hot day. (If desired, add fresh fruit slices before serving.)

FLANNELBOARD FUN

MATERIALS: A flannelboard; green felt; felt scraps; pair of scissors.

PREPARATION: Cut a large cactus shape out of green felt. Cut a small circle out of green felt for the "bump" that grows out of the head of the cactus. Use felt scraps to make a cactus flower shape.

ACTIVITY: Place the cactus shape on your flannelboard. Then read aloud or sing *The Tale of the Old Cactus* and place the other felt shapes on the flannelboard to dramatize the action. When the children have become familiar with the story, let them take turns placing the shapes on the flannelboard.

TOTLINE® BOOKS

PIGGYBACK® SONGS SERIES *Repetition and rhyme*
New songs to the tunes of childhood favorites. No music to read.

Piggyback Songs
A seasonal collection of more than 100 original songs in 64 pages.
WPH 0201

More Piggyback Songs
More seasonal songs—180 in all—in this 96-page collection.
WPH 0202

Piggyback Songs to Sign
Signing phrases to use each month along with new Piggyback songs.
WPH 0209

Holiday Piggyback Songs
More than 250 original songs for 15 holidays and other celebrations.
WPH 0206

Piggyback Songs for School
Delightful songs to use throughout the school day, such as songs for getting acquainted, transitions, storytime, and cleanup.
WPH 0208

Animal Piggyback Songs
More than 200 songs about farm, zoo, and sea animals.
WPH 0207

Piggyback Songs for Infants and Toddlers
A collection of more than 170 songs just right for infants and toddlers. Also appropriate for children ages 3 to 5.
WPH 0203

1•2•3 SERIES
These books emphasize beginning hands-on activities—creative art, no-lose games, puppets, and more. Designed for children ages 3 to 6.

1•2•3 Art
Open-ended art activities emphasizing the creative process are included in this 160-page book. All 238 activities use inexpensive, readily available materials.
WPH 0401

1•2•3 Games
Each of the 70 no-lose games in this book are designed to foster creativity and decision making for a variety of ages.
WPH 0402

1•2•3 Colors
160 pages of activities for "Color Days," including art, learning games, language, science, movement, music, and snacks.
WPH 0403

1•2•3 Science
Fun, wonder-filled activities to get children excited about science and help develop early science skills such as predicting and estimating.
WPH 0410

1•2•3 Rhymes, Songs & Stories
Capture the imaginations of young children with these open-ended rhymes, songs, and stories.
WPH 0408

1•2•3 Puppets
More than 50 simple puppets to make for working with young children, including Willie Worm, Dancing Spoon, and more.
WPH 0404

1•2•3 Math
This book has activities galore for experiencing number concepts such as sorting, measuring, time, and ages.
WPH 0409

1•2•3 Reading & Writing
Ideas for meaningful and non-threatening activities help young children develop *pre-reading* and *pre-writing* skills.
WPH 0407

1001 SERIES
These super reference books are filled with just the right solution, prop, or poem to get your projects going. Creative, inexpensive ideas await you in these resources for parents and teachers of young children.

1001 Teaching Tips
Busy teachers on limited budgets will appreciate these 1001 short-cuts to success! Three major sections include curriculum tips, room tips, and special times tips. Plus a subject index!
WPH 1502

1001 Rhymes & Fingerplays
A complete language resource for parents and teachers! Rhymes for all occasions, plus poems about self-esteem, families, the environment, special needs, and more.
WPH 1503

1001 Teaching Props
The ultimate how-to prop book! A comprehensive materials index makes it easy to create projects by using available recyclable materials. Now it's easy and fun to plan projects and equip centers.
WPH 1501

TOTLINE BOOKS

SNACK SERIES

A most delicious series of books that provides healthy opportunities for fun and learning.

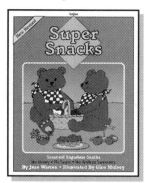

Super Snacks

This revised edition includes nutritional information for CACFP programs and recipes for treats that contain no sugar, honey, or artificial sweeteners!
WPH 1601

Healthy Snacks

Over 100 recipes for healthy alternatives to junk-food snacks! Each recipe is low in fat, sugar, and sodium.
WPH 1602

Teaching Snacks

This book promotes the teaching of basic skills and concepts through cooking. Extend learning into snacktime!
WPH 1603

6/94

THEME-A-SAURUS® SERIES

These books are handy, instant resources for those moments when you need to expand curiosity into meaningful learning experiences. Each book covers around-the-curriculum activities.

Theme-A-Saurus

Grab instant action with more than 50 themes from Apples to Zebras, and more than 600 activity ideas.
WPH 1001

Theme-A-Saurus II

New opportunities for hands-on learning with 60 more theme units that range from Ants to Zippers.
WPH 1002

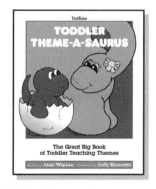

Toddler Theme-A-Saurus

Capture the attention of toddlers with 60 teaching themes that combine safe and appropriate materials with creative activity ideas.
WPH 1003

Alphabet Theme-A-Saurus

Giant letter recognition units are filled with hands-on activities that introduce young children to the ABCs.
WPH 1004

Nursery Rhyme Theme-A-Saurus

Capture children's enthusiasm with nursery rhymes and related learning activities in this 160-page book.
WPH 1005

Storytime Theme-A-Saurus

This book combines 12 storytime favorites with fun and meaningful hands-on activities and songs.
WPH 1006

BUSY BEES SERIES

Fun for Two's and Three's
Hands-on projects and movement games are just right for busy hands and feet of two- and three-year-olds!

NEW! Busy Bees—Fall

Attention-getting activities with a fun fall agenda! Includes simple songs, rhymes, snacks, movements, art, and science projects.
WPH 2405

NEW!
PLAY & LEARN SERIES

Hands-on activities explore the versatile play and learn opportunities of a familiar object. For ages 3 to 8.

Play & Learn with Magnets

Fun and inexpensive ideas for using magnets in learning games, art, storytime, and science.
WPH 2301

Play & Learn with Rubber Stamps

Around-the-curriculum fun with simple rubber stamps. Perfect for ages 3 to 8.
WPH 2302

EXPLORING SERIES

Environments
Instill the spirit of exploration with these beginning science books that let you take activities as far as your children's interest will go.

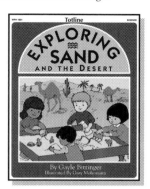

Exploring Sand and the Desert

Set up a child-directed learning environment with this resource. Contains hands-on activity suggestions for learning at the sand table and about the desert environment and how to preserve it.
WPH 1801

Exploring Water and the Ocean

This 96-page book is water fun at its best. Offers a full around-the-curriculum unit using water, plus an introduction to the ocean environment with an emphasis on preservation.
WPH 1802

Exploring Wood and the Forest

This guide for a child-directed learning environment includes activities for developing early carpentry skills and acquiring knowledge about forests.
WPH 1803

Totline®

Instant hands-on ideas for early childhood educators & parents!

This newsletter offers challenging and creative hands-on activities for ages 2 to 6. Each bimonthly issue includes • seasonal fun • learning games • open-ended art • music and movement • language activities • science fun • reproducible patterns and • reproducible parent-flyer pages. Every activity is designed to make maximum use of common, inexpensive materials.

Sample issue $2

Individual and Group Subscriptions Available

Sample issue $1

Individual and Reproducible Subscriptions Available

Super Snack News

Nutritious food, facts and fun!

This monthly newsletter features four pages of healthy recipes, nutrition tips, and related songs and activities for young children. Also provided are portion guidelines for the CACFP government program. Sharing *Super Snack News* is a wonderful way to help promote quality childcare. A Reproducible Subscription allows you the right to make up to 200 copies.